WAR OF THE WEEDS
published by Gold 'n' Honey Books
a division of Multnomah Publishers, Inc.

© 1998 by Multnomah Publishers, Inc.
Illustrations © 1998 by David Harto

International Standard Book Number: 1-57673-308-4

Printed in Mexico.

For information:
MULTNOMAH PUBLISHERS, INC.
POST OFFICE BOX 1720
SISTERS, OREGON 97759

Library of Congress Cataloging-in-Publication Data:
Carlson, Melody.
The war of the weeds / by Melody Carlson ; illustrated by David Harto.
p. cm.
ISBN 1-57673-308-4 (alk. paper)
1. Tares (Parable)—Juvenile literature. I. Harto, David, ill. II. Title.
BT378.T34C37 1998
226.8'09505—dc21   97–45005
                                                     CIP
                                                     AC

98 99 00 01 02 03 04 — 10 9 8 7 6 5 4 3 2 1

A FRUIT TROOP ADVENTURE

WAR OF THE WEEDS

By Melody Carlson • Illustrated by David Harto

Welcome to Fruitville, home of the Fruit Troop. There's no other place like it in all the earth! Fruitville is special because the Gardener watches over it. Sunshine spills over the rooftops and yards nearly every day. Bright flowers in tidy gardens nod their heads in time with the friendly breeze. And it rains just often enough to keep everything green and growing.

The Fruit Troopers live happily together as long as they remember to do what the Gardener has taught them: to love and obey the Gardener and to love others as much as they love themselves. But sometimes the Fruit Troopers forget. And then you can't tell what might happen!

One day, a strange plant popped up in Fruitville, smack in the middle of Anna Apple's yard. Anna bent down to get a closer look.

"Tammy, come and look at this," Anna called. "I've never seen a plant like this! It grew overnight."

"Wow!" exclaimed Tammy Tangerine. "It's different than the other plants in Fruitville. Look, it has little white flowers. What do you think it is?"

"I don't know. I've never heard of a flower that could grow up overnight. I wonder if—nah, it couldn't be. The little white flowers remind me of apple blossoms."

"Hmm," said Tammy. "They remind *me* of tangerine blossoms."

They both giggled.

By the next morning, Anna's strange plant had grown much larger. And white flowers were popping out everywhere.

"Hi, Anna," Penny called from across the street.

"Come and see my new flower," said Anna. "I don't know what it is, but it sure is growing fast."

Penny knelt down to examine the plant. "Oh, dear," she said gently. "This isn't a flower. This is a *weed*."

"But it's so pretty," said Anna with a frown. "It can't be a weed."

"It might look pretty right now, but it will grow and spread, and before long there

will be weeds everywhere. You don't want that to happen."

"I don't know why not," Anna argued. "I think they're pretty."

Penny just shook her head. "Weeds are weeds, Anna. Remember what the Gardener told us? If we see something bad in our lives, we need to get rid of it right away."

"Well, I don't think these little white flowers are bad," Anna insisted. "I think you're just jealous because you want to have the best flower garden in Fruitville and you don't have any of these flowers. I'm not pulling them. So there!"

Penny shook her head and went home.

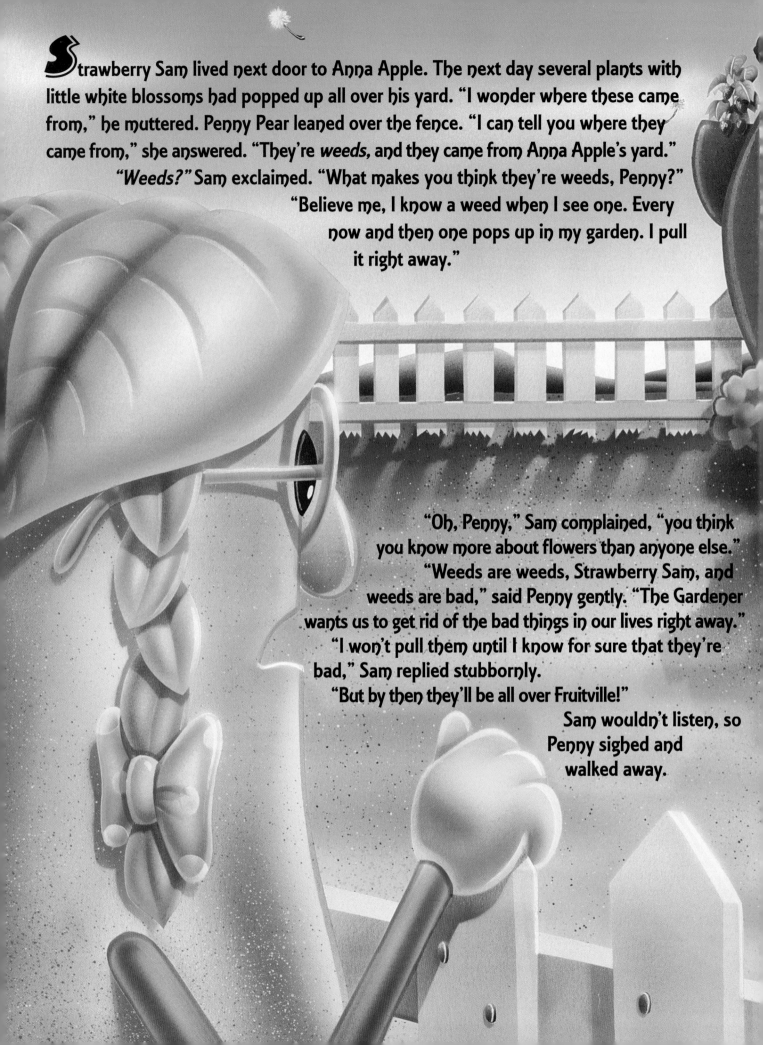

Strawberry Sam lived next door to Anna Apple. The next day several plants with little white blossoms had popped up all over his yard. "I wonder where these came from," he muttered. Penny Pear leaned over the fence. "I can tell you where they came from," she answered. "They're *weeds,* and they came from Anna Apple's yard." *"Weeds?"* Sam exclaimed. "What makes you think they're weeds, Penny?" "Believe me, I know a weed when I see one. Every now and then one pops up in my garden. I pull it right away."

"Oh, Penny," Sam complained, "you think you know more about flowers than anyone else." "Weeds are weeds, Strawberry Sam, and weeds are bad," said Penny gently. "The Gardener wants us to get rid of the bad things in our lives right away." "I won't pull them until I know for sure that they're bad," Sam replied stubbornly. "But by then they'll be all over Fruitville!"

Sam wouldn't listen, so Penny sighed and walked away.

Strawberry Sam, Anna Apple, and Tammy Tangerine marveled at the strange plants with their little white flowers. The other Fruit Troopers tried to get them to pull the weeds, but they wouldn't listen. They were a tiny bit worried at how quickly the plants were spreading, but they didn't want to admit it. So they pretended to be happy when the flowers turned into fluffy white puffballs that blew all over Fruitville.

"Aren't they fun?" cried Tammy. "They look like tiny parachutes!"

"Or fuzzy snowflakes," said Strawberry Sam.

"There are so many that they look like clouds!" Anna added as the weed seeds spread far and wide.

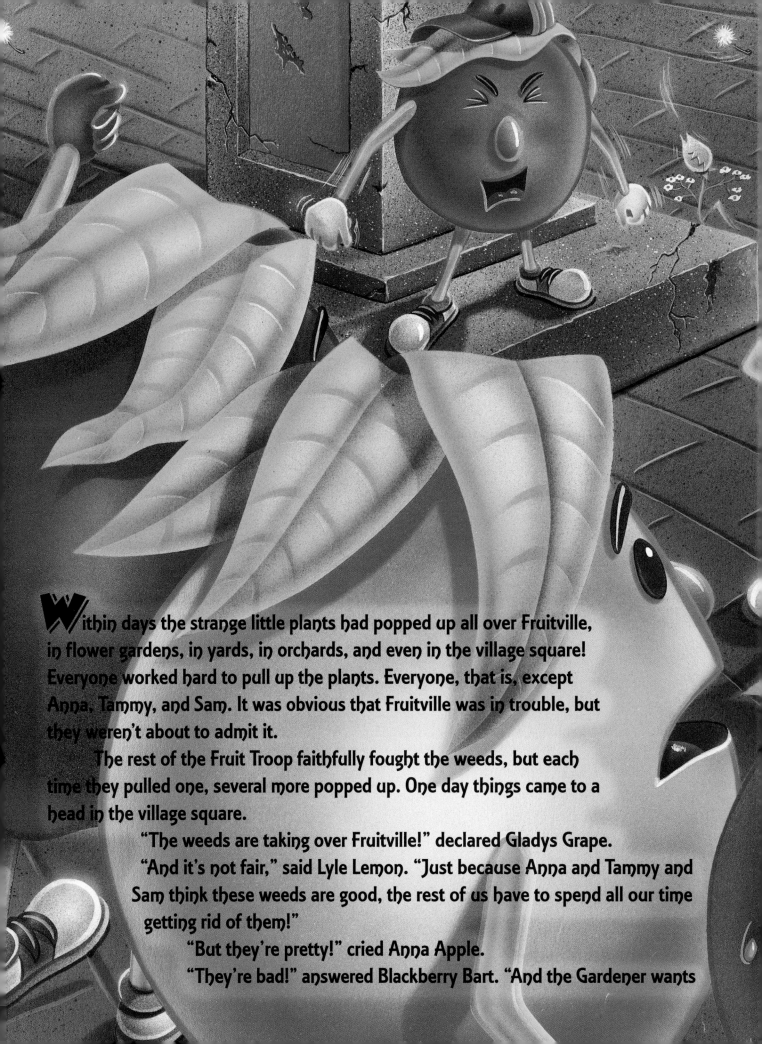

Within days the strange little plants had popped up all over Fruitville, in flower gardens, in yards, in orchards, and even in the village square! Everyone worked hard to pull up the plants. Everyone, that is, except Anna, Tammy, and Sam. It was obvious that Fruitville was in trouble, but they weren't about to admit it.

The rest of the Fruit Troop faithfully fought the weeds, but each time they pulled one, several more popped up. One day things came to a head in the village square.

"The weeds are taking over Fruitville!" declared Gladys Grape.

"And it's not fair," said Lyle Lemon. "Just because Anna and Tammy and Sam think these weeds are good, the rest of us have to spend all our time getting rid of them!"

"But they're pretty!" cried Anna Apple.

"They're bad!" answered Blackberry Bart. "And the Gardener wants

us to get rid of bad things in our lives."

"But their little parachutes are fun," insisted Tammy Tangerine.

"Weeds are weeds," said Penny Pear.

Before long the argument got so loud that no one could hear what anyone else was saying.

"Quiet," said Peachy Pete. But no one would listen.

And so the war of the weeds began. Blackberry Bart called for volunteers to organize a weed patrol. Everyone pitched in and gathered shovels, hoes, rakes, and wheelbarrows. Together they fought to get rid of the weeds. But it was a losing battle. Pineapple Paul began to run out of patience. And Gladys Grape's joy shriveled like a raisin in the sun. Penny Pear knelt by her garden and sobbed; the weeds had choked out all her lovely flowers!

Though they tried with all their might, the weed patrol could not win the war of the weeds. As long as Sam, Anna, and Tammy allowed weeds to grow in their yards, the weed patrol would never be able to keep up. Would this be the end of Fruitville?

The next afternoon, Gladys Grape invited the weed patrol to meet at her house.

"I don't know what more we can do," sighed Lyle Lemon.

"I'm all out of patience," said Pineapple Paul.

"There's no way to make peace," said Peachy Pete.

"Goodness grapes!" said Gladys. "Here comes Strawberry Sam!"

"Hi," said Sam meekly. "I'm joining the weed patrol. I'm getting berry tired of all those pesky white flowers."

"They're not flowers, Sam," said Penny gently. "They're weeds."

Sam nodded sadly. "I'm sorry I didn't believe you. It didn't take me long to see that I was wrong; I just couldn't admit it. I wouldn't blame you for being mad at me."

"We forgive you, Sam," said Peachy Pete. "Now we need to convince Tammy and Anna."

Sam shook his head. "I talked to them just before I came, but they wouldn't listen."

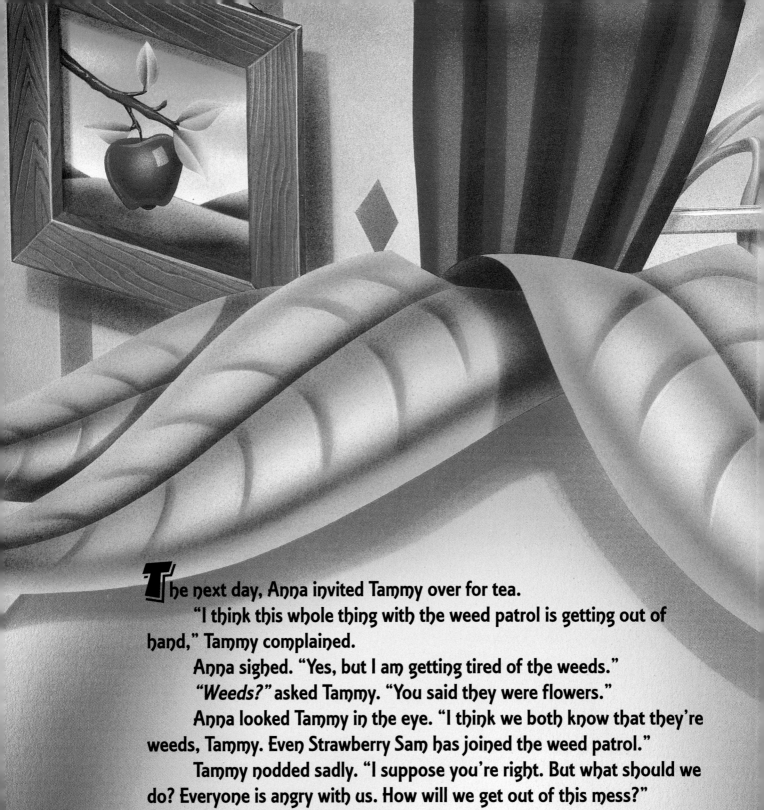

The next day, Anna invited Tammy over for tea.

"I think this whole thing with the weed patrol is getting out of hand," Tammy complained.

Anna sighed. "Yes, but I am getting tired of the weeds."

"*Weeds?*" asked Tammy. "You said they were flowers."

Anna looked Tammy in the eye. "I think we both know that they're weeds, Tammy. Even Strawberry Sam has joined the weed patrol."

Tammy nodded sadly. "I suppose you're right. But what should we do? Everyone is angry with us. How will we get out of this mess?"

Anna looked out her window. "Speaking of getting out, have you noticed that it's getting dark in here?"

"Oh no!" cried Tammy. "The weeds have completely covered the house."

When Anna tried to open the door, it wouldn't budge. Tammy pushed on the window, but the weeds had wrapped it shut.

"We're trapped!" sobbed Tammy.

"Weed patrol alert! Weed patrol alert!" cried Blackberry Bart as he ran through the streets of Fruitville.

"What is it?" asked Peachy Pete. "We're too tired to battle any weeds right now."

"Tammy and Anna need our help!" explained Bart as the others gathered around to hear. "The Gardener told me that they're trapped in Anna's house. The weeds have covered the house completely and they can't get out."

"Leaping lemons!" cried Lyle. "That's a sour situation."

"Fruit Troopers, grab your hoes!" ordered Blackberry Bart.

"We're off to the rescue!" shouted Pineapple Paul.

So the Fruit Troopers gathered their equipment and marched off to Anna Apple's house.

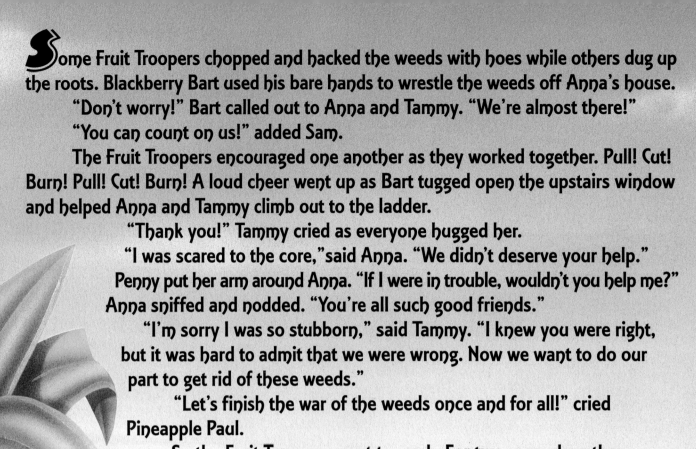

Some Fruit Troopers chopped and hacked the weeds with hoes while others dug up the roots. Blackberry Bart used his bare hands to wrestle the weeds off Anna's house.

"Don't worry!" Bart called out to Anna and Tammy. "We're almost there!"

"You can count on us!" added Sam.

The Fruit Troopers encouraged one another as they worked together. Pull! Cut! Burn! Pull! Cut! Burn! A loud cheer went up as Bart tugged open the upstairs window and helped Anna and Tammy climb out to the ladder.

"Thank you!" Tammy cried as everyone hugged her.

"I was scared to the core," said Anna. "We didn't deserve your help."

Penny put her arm around Anna. "If I were in trouble, wouldn't you help me?"

Anna sniffed and nodded. "You're all such good friends."

"I'm sorry I was so stubborn," said Tammy. "I knew you were right, but it was hard to admit that we were wrong. Now we want to do our part to get rid of these weeds."

"Let's finish the war of the weeds once and for all!" cried Pineapple Paul.

So the Fruit Troopers went to work. For two more days they bravely attacked the menacing weeds. They worked together until the last nasty weed shriveled in the fire.

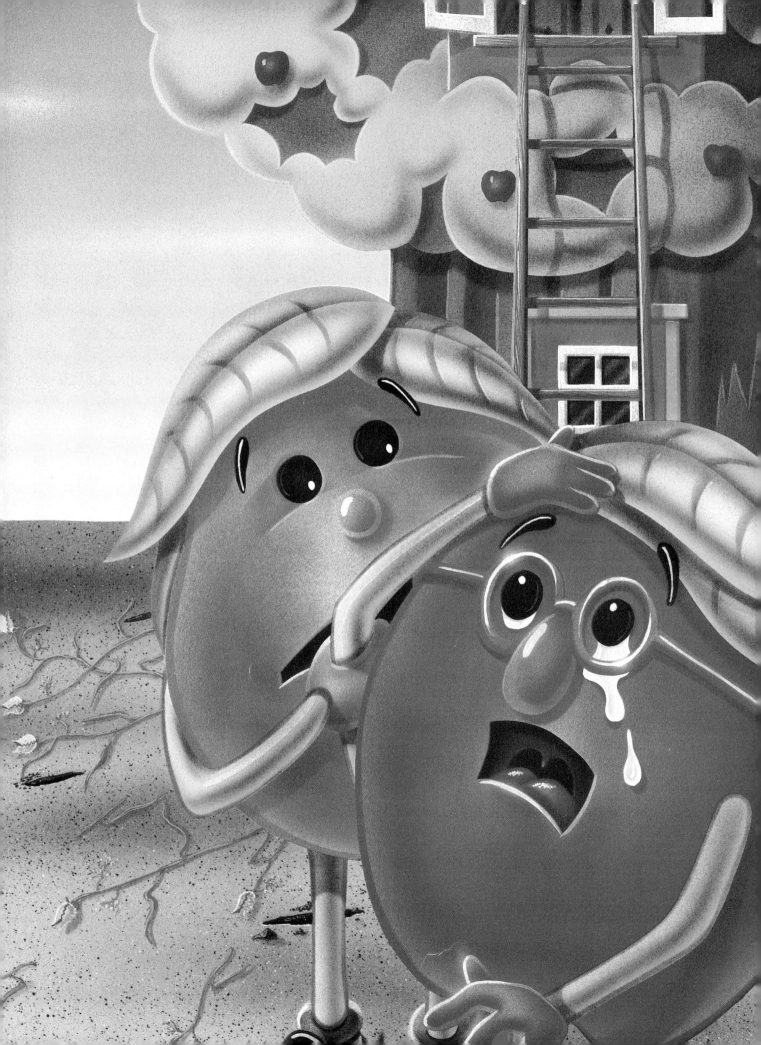

Just then the Gardener appeared.

"You've done well, Fruit Troopers," he said in a quiet voice. "I'm proud of the way you worked together."

Anna and Tammy were a little nervous.

"I'm sorry, Gardener," said Tammy. "I knew almost from the very beginning that the weeds were bad."

"Me too," added Anna. "But it was hard to admit we were wrong. You've told us that when we have something bad in our lives, we should get rid of it right away. We disobeyed."

"I forgive you," the Gardener said with a smile. "It took courage to admit you were wrong. And you worked hard to make things right."

"We've learned a lesson we'll never forget," Tammy said as the Gardener gave her a big hug.

Then Anna spoke to the whole group. "Sam and Tammy and I would like to host a victory celebration tomorrow in the village square. You're all invited!"

And what a celebration it was! There were enough pies and cookies and sweets to give everyone a toothache. Gladys Grape gave Blackberry Bart a special medal for his brave rescue of Tammy and Anna.

Then Strawberry Sam cleared his throat and said, "Penny Pear has written a special poem for this happy occasion."

Penny Pear stood before the crowd and read:

Weeds may come in lots of shapes,
In different colors and sizes.
And though they may seem nice at first
They're full of bad surprises.

When bad things come into our lives
At first, they may seem nice.
But if we don't get rid of them,
We'll pay an awful price.

The Gardener teaches us what's right;
We listen and obey.
We love and care for all our friends,
That's the Fruit Troop way!

Melody Carlson, a former preschool teacher, holds a degree in early childhood education and has many years of experience in working with young children. She is the author of the *Gold & Honey Bible, Tupsu, The Ark that Noah Built,* and *The Sea Hag's Treasure.* She has also published numerous short stories in teen and children's periodicals and has won fiction writing awards. Melody lives with her husband and family in Oregon. They enjoy skiing, hiking, and boating in the beautiful Cascades.

David Harto, pictured here with his cat, Audrey, studied illustration at the Art Institute of Seattle. He has been a freelance commercial illustrator for the last fifteen years, working with such clients as Nintendo, K2 Skis, Microsoft, and Lands' End. David frequently teaches illustration at the School of Visual Concepts. He and his wife, Nancy, make their home in Ballard, Washington. When he's not drawing, he's building something with his hands or doing the thing he loves most in the world: being with his son, Roman, who just recently came into his life.